UNANANA
AND THE ENORMOUS
ELEPHANT

and

The Feathered Snake

Retold by MARGARET MAYO
Illustrated by PETER BAILEY

ORCHARD BOOKS

For Natalie
M.M.
With love to the two young whippersnappers,
Oscar and Felix
P.B.

Orchard Books
96 Leonard Street, London EC2A 4XD
Orchard Books Australia
32/45-51 Huntley Street, Alexandria, NSW 2015
The text was first published in Great Britain in the form
of a gift collection called *The Orchard Book of Magical Tales*
and *The Orchard Book of Mythical Birds and Beasts*
illustrated by Jane Ray, in 1993 and 1996
This edition first published in hardback in 2003
First paperback publication in 2004
The Orchard Book of Magical Tales Text © Margaret Mayo 1993
The Orchard Book of Mythical Birds and Beasts Text © Margaret Mayo 1996
Illustrations © Peter Bailey 2003
The rights of Margaret Mayo to be identified as the author
and Peter Bailey to be identified as the illustrator of this work have
been asserted by them in accordance with the
Copyright, Designs and Patents Act, 1988.
A CIP catalogue record for this book is available from the British Library
ISBN 1 84362 079 0 (hardback)
ISBN 1 84362 087 1 (paperback)
1 3 5 7 9 10 8 6 4 2 (hardback)
1 3 5 7 9 10 8 6 4 2 (paperback)
Printed in Great Britain

CONTENTS

UNANANA
AND THE ENORMOUS
ELEPHANT

Here is a story – a story about Unanana who one day decided to build a house for herself and her two children, a little boy and a little girl. And she built her house, and she built it well. *But* she built the house in the middle of a wide road, and that road was the animals' road through the bush.

Everyone said, "You can't live there. That is the elephants' road...the leopards' road...the antelopes' road. All the animals use that road. It is a dangerous place."

But Unanana said, "This is a good place to live. I am Unanana and I am not afraid."

Now Unanana's children were beautiful. *Everyone* who saw them said, "Unanana, you have remarkably beautiful children."

And she always answered, "That is true. They are beautiful, and I love them better than anything in the world."

One morning Unanana had to go into the bush to collect firewood, so she asked the children's big cousin, who was staying with them for a few days, to look after the little boy and the little girl. And all three went out and played together on the road while Unanana went off into the bush.

Not long after, a shy, gentle-eyed antelope came leaping along the road, and when she saw the children, she asked, "Whose children are those?"

And Big Cousin answered, "They are Unanana's children."

"Oh!" said the antelope. "They are beautiful, beautiful children!" And she went on her way.

A little while later, a bold, yellow-eyed leopard came prowling along the road, and when she saw the children, she asked, "Whose children are those?"

And Big Cousin answered, "They are Unanana's children."

"Oh!" said the leopard. "They are beautiful, beautiful children!" And she went on her way.

Then, a little while later, an enormous, one-tusked elephant came trampling along the road, and when he saw the children, he asked, "Whose children are those?"

And Big Cousin answered, "They are Unanana's children."

"Au! Au!" trumpeted the elephant.
"They are beautiful, beautiful children!
But they are playing in the middle of
MY road!"

And – next thing – he stretched out his
long trunk and picked up the little boy
and swooshed him right into his mouth.
Gulp! Gulp! He swallowed him whole.

Then he stretched
out that long trunk
again and picked
up the little girl
and swooshed her
right into his
mouth. *Gulp!*
Gulp! He swallowed
her whole. And, yet again, he stretched out
that long trunk. But Big Cousin wasn't
there. Fast, fast, *very fast* she had run into
the house and closed the door behind her.

Then, swinging his long, stretchy trunk
from side to side, the enormous, one-
tusked elephant went on his way.

When Unanana came home with the
firewood, the first thing she noticed was
that her children were not playing outside.
She went into the house, and there was Big
Cousin hunched up in a corner, crying.

"Where are my beautiful children?" asked Unanana.

"They have been taken by an enormous, one-tusked elephant," said Big Cousin.

"What did he do with them?" asked Unanana.

"He ate them," said Big Cousin.

"Did he swallow them whole?" asked Unanana.

"I don't know," said Big Cousin.

Then Unanana ground some maize and mixed it with some milk and cooked a delicious creamy porridge in a large pot. And when the porridge had cooled, she put the pot full of porridge on her head, picked up a big, sharp knife and off she went.

11

She marched along the animals' road, and she marched and she marched, until she met a shy, gentle-eyed antelope.

"Good mother antelope," said Unanana, "where can I find the enormous, one-tusked elephant that has eaten my beautiful children?"

And the antelope said, "You must go and go and keep going until you come to the place of tall trees and white stones."

So Unanana marched along the animals' road, and she marched and she marched, until she met a bold, yellow-eyed leopard.

"Good mother leopard," she said, "where can I find the enormous, one-tusked elephant that has eaten my beautiful children?"

And the leopard said, "You must go and go and keep going until you come to the place of tall trees and white stones."

So Unanana marched along the animals' road, and she marched and she marched, until she saw an enormous, one-tusked elephant lying down under some tall trees, and all around him were piles of white stones.

Unanana marched up to the elephant and she said, "Are you the elephant that ate my beautiful children?"

The elephant said, "No, I am not the one! Go and go and keep going, and you will find the elephant."

Unanana shouted, *"Are you the elephant that ate my beautiful children?"*

The elephant said, "No, of course I am not the one! Go and go and keep going, and you will find the elephant."

Then Unanana bellowed, "ARE YOU THE ELEPHANT THAT ATE MY BEAUTIFUL CHILDREN?"

And the elephant, still lying on the ground, stretched out his long trunk and picked up Unanana and swooshed her right into his mouth. *Gulp! Gulp!* He swallowed her whole, together with the pot full of delicious creamy porridge and the big, sharp knife.

When Unanana got inside the elephant,
she *was* surprised. The place was full of
dogs, goats, cattle and a whole lot of
people – just sitting there, all slumpish
and sorry for themselves.

But Unanana didn't sit down. She
marched up and down, round and
round, inside the elephant, until – *such
great happiness!* – she found her two

beautiful children sitting next to each
other, holding hands.

"Have you had anything to eat?"
she asked.

"No," they said, both together. "And
we are so hungry."

"Well," said Unanana, "I have
brought you some delicious creamy
porridge."

17

By the time the children had eaten
as much porridge as they wanted, every
single person and every single animal
inside the elephant had
jumped up and
gathered round.
They were
very hungry.
So Unanana shared
out the rest of the food;
and there was some for everyone.

Now, what with Unanana marching up
and down and all the
people and animals
jumping up and
gathering round
her, the enormous,
one-tusked elephant
began to feel
uncomfortable.

"Stop moving around down there!"
he shouted. "You're giving me a pain in
the stomach!"

Unanana said, "Stop moving, indeed!
Come on, everybody, let's dance!"

So then the dogs, the goats, the cattle
and all the people began to dance.

"Au! Au!" trumpeted the elephant.
He had such a big pain in his stomach.
"Au! Au! Au! Stop dancing down there!"
But they danced and danced.

The elephant thought to himself, "Since the moment I swallowed that woman, I haven't had any peace! This is too much!" And he shouted, "Get out, all of you! Get out!"

"And how can we get out?" Unanana called back.

"Any way you like!" shouted the elephant. "That's how!"

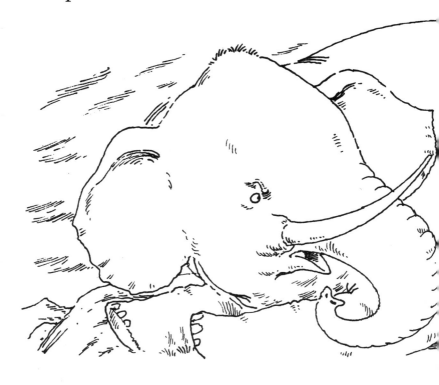

Then Unanana said, "There is only one way." And she took her big, sharp knife and cut a doorway in the side of the elephant.

And out skipped the dogs and the goats and the cattle, barking and bleating and mooing; and out skipped all the people, laughing. They were so glad to see the grass and the trees and the sky again.

The animals all thanked Unanana
for saving them, and hurried off home.
And then the people thanked her. But,
before hurrying home, they all promised
to come and visit her one day at her house
in the middle of the animals' road.

Meanwhile, the enormous, one-tusked elephant just lay there. Even though he had a wound in his side, he was glad to see those animals and people – most especially Unanana! – hurrying away. He didn't want to see them ever again. They had given him such a big pain in his stomach.

When Unanana and her two children came home and Big Cousin saw them, there was *such great happiness*! Then Unanana ground some maize and mixed it with some milk and cooked another pot of creamy porridge, and they sat down together and ate it. And it did taste good.

From then on, it was never quiet
at Unanana's house, because the people
she had met inside the elephant, and
the parents of the children who had
been there, all came to visit her.

And every time the visitors came, they
brought presents – a cow or a goat –
something like that. And so Unanana
and her beautiful children became rich.

25

But they still lived in their house in the middle of the animals' road. Unanana liked it there. And the enormous, one-tusked elephant? He never ever came back.

A Zulu tale from South Africa

THE
FEATHERED
SNAKE

In the beginning times there was no
music on earth. No one knew how to
sing. Not even the birds. But there *was*
music, far away and high above, in the
House of the Sun.

One day the great god Smoking
Mirror came to earth and walked about,
examining the things he had helped
to make.

"Very good! Everything looks just the way I wanted," he said. "The flowers, the birds, the animals! Bright colours everywhere! And yet…I feel something is missing." He listened. He walked on and listened some more. "I *know* what's missing," he said.

He threw back his head and hurled his voice to the four quarters of the earth. "Come, Quetzal-co-atl, feathered snake, restless Lord of the Winds! Come! I need you!"

Quetzalcoatl was a long way off, drifting lazily above the waves, but he heard. He lifted his snake head and opened his mouth wide, until a human face appeared within his jaws. It was a rather grumpy face.

"It's always the same," he grumbled.
"Just when I'm enjoying a rest, I'm
wanted for something or other. Still,
I suppose I must go and find out what's
the matter now!"

He gathered himself together, his glossy
feathers rippling around him, changing
colour, now green, now turquoise, now
blue...and then he came flying.

Fast, faster than
fast, he flew.
Waves rose high.
They crashed
down on the shore.
Trees lifted their
branches and tossed

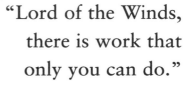

them to and fro. In a great whoosh of
sound, he landed beside Smoking Mirror.

"So – what do you want?" asked
Quetzalcoatl. He was brisk and sharp.

Those two were not always friends. It

didn't take much for
them to quarrel.
But Smoking Mirror
was cunning. He spoke
softly, flatteringly.
"Lord of the Winds,
there is work that
only you can do."

"Wo-rk!" Quetzalcoatl howled out the word. "I wouldn't have come if…"

"Listen," said Smoking Mirror. "This bright earth we made together is sick. Listen. Can't you hear? There is no music. And what is life without music? The earth *must* have music. So, feathered snake, great Lord of the Winds, you must go to the House of the Sun and bring some music down to the earth."

"Go to the Sun! Go and get music!" said Quetzalcoatl. "You know the Sun. He loves music. But he's mean. He won't share. He wants every note of music and every single musician for himself alone!"

"But think of the birds, the trees and the moving water," said Smoking Mirror. "Think of the mothers with their babies, lively children, sleepy children, grown men and women. They must have music. *All life* should be full of music!"

Quetzalcoatl thought. "I will go," he said. "I will go to the House of the Sun." He gathered himself together and flew upwards.

Up and up, he flew. He soared through the blue smoke of the sky and on through the empty space. He came to the roof of the world, and then he heard the sound of distant music. He rose up the stairway of light that led to the House of the Sun, and the music grew louder and louder, until he could hear clearly the glorious sound of huge choirs singing and sweet flutes playing.

At last he entered the House of the Sun
and saw the musicians.

They circled the Sun in a nest of light.
There was not a dark colour anywhere.
Each musician was dressed according
to the music played. Those who sang
lullabies and other songs for children
were dressed in white. Those who sang
tender love songs wore deep blue,
while the ones who sang loud songs

about brave deeds and battles were dressed in blood red. But brightest of all were the flute players, who were dressed in a golden yellow that gleamed like the Sun.

The music wove in and out and around the nest of light, as first one group sang and then another played their flutes or maybe sang. The glorious sounds never stopped. Not for a moment.

As soon as he saw him, the Sun knew why Quetzalcoatl had come. "Musicians, be quiet!" ordered the Sun. "Here comes that bothersome nuisance, the feathered one! Don't answer when he speaks or he will steal you away and take you to that terrible, dark, sad place called earth, where there is no music."

For the first time the musicians were silent. They were afraid. They tried not to listen as Quetzalcoatl drifted among them, whispering in their ears: "Take pity on the people of earth. Come with me and teach them how to make music. Come...come..."

Though he pleaded and pleaded, the musicians stood still and silent as statues.

Quetzalcoatl's anger came bubbling up. He coiled himself tight. He uncoiled. He piled up black storm clouds until the Sun's light was covered. He brewed up a hurricane. Lightning flashed. Thunder rumbled and roared.

The musicians were so scared by now!
They had never known darkness like this
before, and they had never been at the
centre of a storm. They ran this way and
that, trying to find the Sun, and some, not
knowing where they were, ran straight
into Quetzalcoatl's feathered embrace.

When he had got hold of some musicians of every kind, he wound his body round them, and slowly and gently, so as not to harm them, he floated down to earth.

Smoking Mirror was there to welcome them as they landed. "Quetzalcoatl," he said, "you have brought such a marvellous flutter of happiness to earth!"

The musicians were so glad when they saw that the earth was not a dark, terrible place after all. It was full of bright colours, and they could still see the Sun, shining above. It was true there was no music, but they could change that.

Swiftly they walked off to the four quarters of the earth, and on their way they taught everyone they met how to sing or how to make flutes and play them.

They also taught the birds to sing, and showed them how to greet the Sun each morning in a loud dawn chorus.

They gave music to the moving water and the rustling leaves.

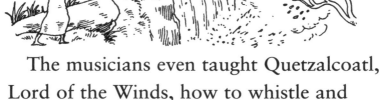

The musicians even taught Quetzalcoatl, Lord of the Winds, how to whistle and sigh and laugh and sing.

And so now, today, all the earth, everywhere, is full of the happiness which music brings!

An Aztec tale from Mexico

UNANANA AND THE ENORMOUS ELEPHANT

A Zulu Tale from South Africa

Elephants are known to make well-defined roads through the African bush, and the male, when angry, is dangerous. They can easily trample people underfoot. The elephant in this story, told by the Zulu tribe (South Africa), has lost a tusk, which suggests he has already been in a fierce fight with another male elephant.

Unanana and the Enormous Elephant is a 'be careful' story, and in some ways is like the European tale *Little Red Riding Hood*. The bush and the woods can be dangerous places for children. The elephant and wolf may appear friendly, but do not trust them. Although neither animal could possibly swallow a human, the stories warn that they might harm you, so 'be careful'.

There are other similarities. In most present day versions of *Little Red Riding Hood*, a brave huntsman kills the wolf and frees the little girl and her grandmother from his stomach. In this Zulu story, Unanana rescues her beautiful children, and everyone else, by her own determination and cleverness.

46

THE FEATHERED SNAKE

An Aztec Tale from Mexico

There are tales from all over the world about the creation of life on earth. In Aztec tales, told in Mexico, the gods Quetzalcoatl and Smoking Mirror – named after his magic mirror in which he could see what was happening anywhere – made the world together.

In *The Feathered Snake,* Smoking Mirror decides the world needs music, but Quetzalcoatl is the one who cleverly captures the sun's musicians and brings them to earth. Stealing something from the sun, for earth's benefit, is also central to a Greek tale. In this story the god, Prometheus, steals fire from the chariot of the sun and brings it to earth so people can use it.

The *quetzal* is a rare bird that lives in the rainforests of Southern Mexico and Guatemala. The male bird has two fantastically long blue-green tail feathers that shimmer as he flies. *Coatl* means snake. Thus, Quetzalcoatl is a feathered snake. Some ancient sculptures depict him as a swirl of long feathers with a snake's head emerging from the top. Inside the open jaws is a human face, while hands and feet can be glimpsed among the feathers.

MAGICAL TALES
from
AROUND THE WORLD

Retold by Margaret Mayo ✳ *Illustrated by Peter Bailey*

PEGASUS AND THE PROUD PRINCE
and The Flying Carpet   ISBN 1 84362 086 3   £3.99

UNANANA AND THE ENORMOUS ELEPHANT
and The Feathered Snake   ISBN 1 84362 087 1   £3.99

THE FIERY PHOENIX
and The Lemon Princess   ISBN 1 84362 088 X   £3.99

THE GIANT SEA SERPENT
and The Unicorn   ISBN 1 84362 089 8   £3.99

THE MAN-EATING MINOTAUR
and The Magic Fruit   ISBN 1 84362 090 1   £3.99

THE MAGICAL MERMAID
and Kate Crackernuts   ISBN 1 84362 091 X   £3.99

THE INCREDIBLE THUNDERBIRD
and Baba Yaga Bony-legs   ISBN 1 84362 092 8   £3.99

THE DARING DRAGON
and The Kingdom Under the Sea   ISBN 1 84362 093 6   £3.99

Orchard Myths are available from all good bookshops,
or can be ordered direct from the publisher:
Orchard Books, PO BOX 29, Douglas IM99 1BQ
Credit card orders please telephone 01624 836000
or fax 01624 837033
or e-mail: bookshop@enterprise.net for details.

To order please quote title, author and ISBN
and your full name and address.
Cheques and postal orders should be
made payable to 'Bookpost plc'.
Postage and packing is FREE within the UK
(overseas customers should add £1.00 per book).

Prices and availability are subject to change.